HAROLD THE HERALD

A Book About Heraldry

Words and Pictures
by Dana Fradon

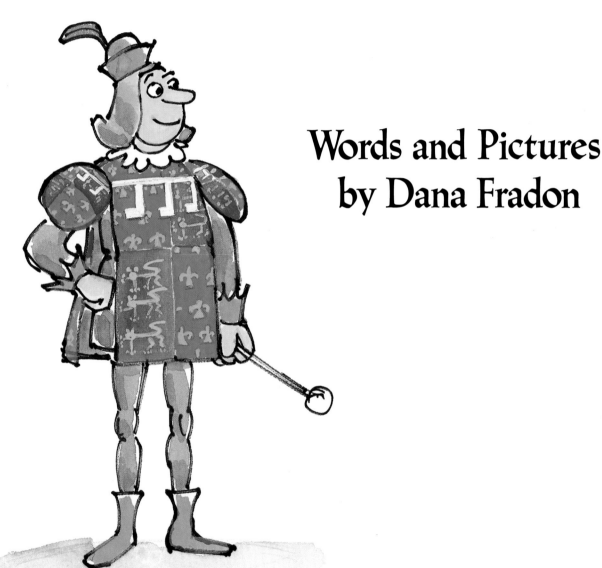

DUTTON CHILDREN'S BOOKS • NEW YORK

AUTHOR'S NOTE

Heraldry is a complex subject. During the some eight hundred years of its formalized existence, its rules have often been bent. Here and there one runs into contradictions. I have used as my final authority a book first published in 1904 titled *The Art of Heraldry—An Encyclopedia of Armory* by Arthur Charles Fox-Davies. To this day, it is still probably the most complete and authoritative book ever written on the subject.

—D.F.

Library of Congress Cataloging-in-Publication Data
Fradon, Dana.
    Harold the herald/by Dana Fradon.—1st ed.
        p.   cm.
    Summary: Miss Quincy's class learns about the duties of a herald in medieval England and the meaning of heraldic symbols.
    ISBN 0-525-44634-6
    1. Heraldry—Juvenile literature.   2. Heraldry—Great Britain—Juvenile literature.   3. Heralds—Great Britain—Juvenile literature.   4. Arms and armor—Juvenile literature.   5. Devices—Juvenile literature.   [1. Heralds.   2. Heraldry. 3. Great Britain—Social life and customs—Medieval period, 1066-1485.]
I. Title.   89-49479
CR21.F74 1990   CIP
929.8′2′0941—dc20   AC

Published in the United States by
Dutton Children's Books,
a division of Penguin Books USA Inc.

Designer: Margo D. Barooshian

Printed in Hong Kong
First Edition   10 9 8 7 6 5 4 3 2 1

To Marion, Albert, Fran, Nick,
Andrew, Melissa, and Sarah

When you come to a colored dot in the text, find the same-colored dot below for a little more information.

● ● ● ●

The students at Hilltop School are getting ready for a visitor. It's no ordinary visitor—it's a suit of armor, six hundred years old. Originally the armor was worn by the knight Sir Dana of Domania. Back then, it *was* an ordinary suit of armor. But now, for some mysterious reason, the armor can talk.

Today the armor is going to talk to students about a man who had a very important job back when Sir Dana was alive. The man was a herald. And his name was Harold. Harold the Herald he was called.

Meanwhile, in a great museum, workers are busy packing the armor into shipping crates. They handle the helmet, the hauberk, ● and the surcoat ● very carefully. The armor is worth at least a million dollars, and they don't want anything to happen to it. A museum guard helps them. He knows the armor well.

When the packing is done, the crates are loaded into a van, which heads for the Hilltop School. The guard keeps a sharp eye out to protect the valuable cargo, and he carries pictures for the armor's talk.

● Armor shirt made of chain mail
● Cloth shirt worn over armor

On the school stage, the workers reassemble the armor. Thongs are tied. Pieces of plate with exotic names like poleyns, greaves, and cuisses ● are buckled and snapped.

The guard recognizes some of the students in the audience, especially the ones from Miss Quincy's class. A few months ago, her class visited the museum, and, to their amazement, they heard the armor talk. Some of them even remember what to do to start the armor up.

● Names for plate armor that protects the knees, thighs, and shins

As the armor stands motionless, the guard asks the students a question.

The guard presses the middle button of his jacket, and the armor begins to speak—

—but, unfortunately, too softly to be heard.

Now the armor speaks loudly enough to be heard by all.

"Greetings, my dear students. It is a pleasure to be here. Today I'm going to tell you about a man named Harold. His name sounds almost like his job, for Harold was a herald.

"What was a herald? Harken ye this! ●

"In medieval times, heralds had many important duties and were always to be found close by their kings, princes, or lords. Heralds helped them govern in war and peace. They helped tell the history of their time. During battle, heralds often lived in their princes' tents. You could say heralds were reporters; military observers; government spokesmen; sportscasters; librarians; lawyers; publicists; memory wizards; and sometimes, unofficially, even spies—all rolled into one!

"But hold! Let us begin the tale of Harold the Herald.

● Pay attention! Listen!

"Harold was born in London, England, in the year 1342. His father was a successful wool merchant. His mother saw to the managing of the large house they lived in and their several servants. Harold and his sister, Emily, were said to be of gentle birth—a small step below the noble class of barons, lords, and knights.

"Harold's mother taught her two children how to read and write in French and English.

I HOPE SOMEDAY HE WILL BE A WOOL MERCHANT LIKE MYSELF.

GOO! GA! GURGLE, GURGLE!

"When Harold was seven and no longer considered a child, he started school. Classes were held in a church. Because they began early in the morning, when it was still dark, the boys and girls carried candles to see by. School lasted until midafternoon, with a two-hour recess for lunch, play, chores, and rest.

● "I don't think I want to be a wool merchant!"

"Harold's schoolmaster taught him arithmetic, geometry, Latin, and rhetoric.● Harold also read and memorized Bible stories, hymns, prayers, and much poetry.

"At age fourteen Harold became a page ● in the castle of a prince named Lionel. There he learned about castle life, from serving dinner and tending horses to taking care of armor—and more. He often heard the titled guests ● tell tales of adventure in far-off places.

● The art of getting a point across; communicating; persuading
● Medieval for *teacher*
● A young helper
● People with titles; barons, lords, dukes...

"Harold also heard the stories heralds told about their experiences at great tournaments or on battlefields or behind enemy lines. Heralds did not joust for sport or wage war as did knights. But battles and tournaments could not take place without heralds.

"Young Harold was often puzzled by a strange language he heard the heralds use. But he soon began to understand that the language described the designs on knights' shields. Harold even learned a few words of the language, as you will too, if you pay me heed.

"In battle or at tournaments, knights had designs on their shields, surcoats, and banners to let others know who they were. When knights were covered in armor from head to toe, it was almost impossible to tell friend from foe without the help of a shield or banner.

"Armies did not have standard uniforms in Harold's day. Each knight wore his own design, called a coat of arms. It was easy to see these colorful emblazoned designs. ● And knights knew enough heraldry so that rarely was anyone killed because of mistaken identity.

"One day Harold saw one of Prince Lionel's heralds, accompanied by a trumpeter, prepare to deliver a proclamation. Harold admired the herald's proud manner and the way the prince's subjects gave him their attention. He decided right then to become a herald.

● The designs were painted on shields; on banners and surcoats they were embroidered.

"When Harold was twenty, Prince Lionel granted his desire. And why not? Harold was intelligent and honest and had an exceptional memory.

"In an official ceremony, Harold was made an apprentice herald, a pursuivant. Edward, an older herald, held a cup of wine in his right hand and, with his left, led Harold before the prince. Edward wore a herald's coat, or tabard, which bore Prince Lionel's coat of arms. Harold wore a tabard too, only he wore his sideways. Wearing it that way showed that Harold was a pursuivant.

"It was the custom for the herald-to-be to receive a new name from the person he served. Sometimes the new name was taken from the name of a city or town, like the Derby Herald, or from a castle, like the Windsor Herald. Sometimes the new name was the lord's own name. The herald of Sir John Chandos, an English knight, was called simply Chandos Herald.

"Sometimes a pursuivant was renamed by a ruler's whim. ●

● Whatever came into the ruler's mind to say

"One duke renamed his pursuivant 'White Boar,' after the animal that appeared on the duke's shield. So that is what everyone called the herald —White Boar Herald!

"On a whim Prince Lionel decided, 'The pursuivant's name shall remain Harold. I like the sound of Harold the Herald. It near rhymes, and it will be easy to remember.'

"Harold the pursuivant then swore an oath of fealty● to Prince Lionel. And then—by Neptune's beard!●—Harold was baptized by having the wine poured over his head.

● Loyalty
● An expression of surprise

"Scarcely was the new pursuivant dry—Ho! I but jest—when his training began. Under the guidance of the older herald, Edward, Harold studied the thousands of colorful designs emblazoned on knights' shields, surcoats, and banners.

"He learned more of the mysterious-sounding language that he had first heard as a page. Called Blazon, it was a language composed of words from Old French, Old English, Latin, and other languages. Some words even came from the Holy Land and Arabia. Some words were so mysterious that no one is certain of their origins.

"There were seven major colors used on coats of arms. Each color had a special name in Blazon.

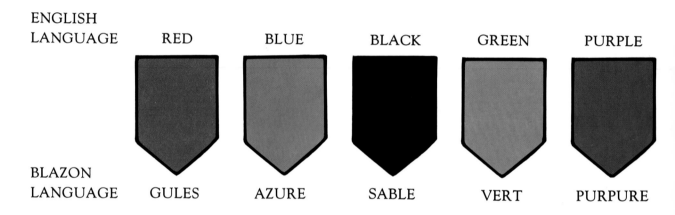

ENGLISH LANGUAGE	RED	BLUE	BLACK	GREEN	PURPLE
BLAZON LANGUAGE	GULES	AZURE	SABLE	VERT	PURPURE

"Two of the seven colors were called metals. ●

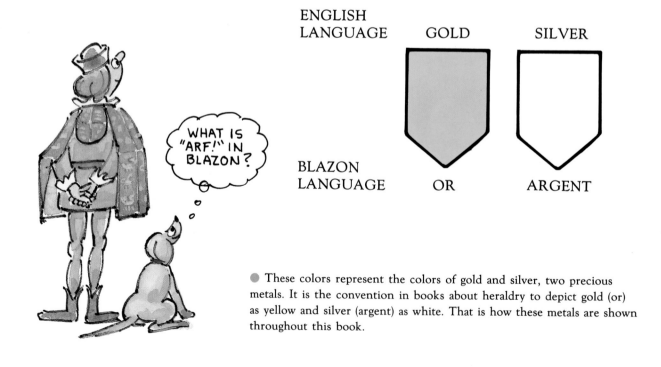

ENGLISH LANGUAGE	GOLD	SILVER
BLAZON LANGUAGE	OR	ARGENT

WHAT IS "ARF!" IN BLAZON?

● These colors represent the colors of gold and silver, two precious metals. It is the convention in books about heraldry to depict gold (or) as yellow and silver (argent) as white. That is how these metals are shown throughout this book.

"There were also two decorative patterns used on coats of arms. Because the patterns were inspired by two small, furry animals, the ermine and the squirrel, they were called furs.

ENGLISH
LANGUAGE

ERMINE FUR

SQUIRREL FUR

BLAZON
LANGUAGE

ERMINE

VAIR

"The ermine is a white animal with a black-tipped tail. When ermine furs were sewed side by side to make linings for cloaks, they formed a pattern that became the basic ermine pattern. Some squirrels are gray with white undersides. Squirrel skins laid side by side formed the basic vair pattern. The furs themselves were not attached to shields—the fur patterns were painted on.

"There are many variations to the basic fur patterns. Here are four—

"In the early days of heraldry, eight hundred years ago, the most common designs on knights' shields were simple, flat decorations. Their broad, colorful shapes could be seen from far away, and they were easy to paint.

"Harold the pursuivant had to memorize twenty-eight basic shapes—and their *thousands* of variations. He knew them all as well as most people know the names of their families and friends. Because these basic shapes were so commonly used, they were called ordinaries and subordinaries. ●

"Here are a handful and their Blazon names.

FESS
The fess is a wide band drawn horizontally across the middle of the shield.

PALE
The pale is a broad vertical band running down the middle of the shield. It represents an upright strip of wood used to form a fence.

CHEVRON
The chevron is an upside-down V. It represents two building rafters that meet at the peak of the roof.

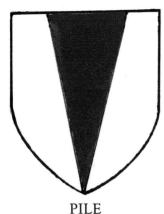

PILE
The pile is a triangle. It represents a dart, arrowhead, or pointed stake.

CROSS
The cross is a symbol that can be traced back to ancient mythology. Since Christ, it has been known mainly as a symbol of Christianity.

SALTIRE
The saltire is one of the four hundred variations of the cross. It is the cross of Saint Andrew, the patron saint of Scotland.

● Ordinaries and subordinaries are equally important shapes.

BORDURE

A bordure is a border around the edge of the shield.

LOZENGE

A lozenge is a diamond taller than it is wide. It often indicates the achievements of a female.

BEND

The bend is a broad band running from top right—the knight's right—to the bottom left. ●

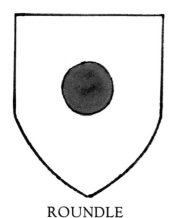

ROUNDLE

A roundle is a circular figure with many names. It is called a bezant when it is gold; a plate when silver; a torteau when red; a hurt when blue; an ogress, pellet, or gunstone when black; a pomeis when green; and a golpe when purple.

SHAKEFORK

The shakefork is a Y-shape, based on the two-pronged pitchfork used to shake and separate grain from straw and husks.

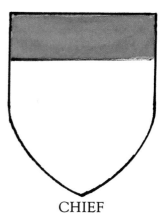

CHIEF

The chief is a band that runs across the top of the shield. It is the head or principal part of the shield.

● The knight's left is called the sinister side, and his right is called the dexter side. When a band runs from the top sinister to the bottom dexter, it is called a bend sinister.

"Down through the ages, animals, birds, and even dragons have appeared on knights' shields, surcoats, and pennants. A medieval Welsh poet believed that each animal on a coat of arms revealed something about the character and temperament of the person who bore it.

"Here are some of the poet's observations, as best I can recall.

"A man with a dog on his shield would be loyal, would never desert his master, and would willingly die for him.

"Fearsome and generous would be a man with an eagle emblem, for that describes the eagle. Upon hearing the eagle's cry, other birds fear to hunt nearby. Yet, when an eagle has eaten its fill, it generously throws what is left to the other birds.

"The cockerel or rooster is a courageous fighter. But upon defeating its opponent, the cock always crows. Obnoxious and ill-mannered, though a valiant warrior, might be the man who wears this bird.

"The medieval poet tells the following story about the bear—

"The bear is a strong but irritable animal. When hungry it likes to steal honey from beehives. Often, to prevent this, a beekeeper would hang a heavy mallet at the hive entrance. When the bear swatted it away to get at the honey, the mallet would swing back just as swiftly and strike the bear on the head. Again and again the bear would repeat this futile exercise, until, dizzy from the mallet blows, it staggered off empty-handed.

"A bear on a warrior's shield would indicate a strong, irritable, if slow-witted man—who likes sweets. Hah! I jest about the sweets!

● "I say we drive the bear away by stinging him."
● "Whe-e-e! Lances at the ready!"

"The dragon breathes out fire. The man who bears a dragon on his shield is powerful and so thirsty for battle that even water cannot quench his warlike feelings.

"In heraldry, the dragon's mouth is always shown open to allow the flames inside to escape.

"The lion is the noblest of beasts, its roar much feared. It does not kill people unless hard-pressed by hunger. It shares its prey with other animals that follow it around, awaiting its generosity.

"A lion on a shield indicates a strong, brave, even ferocious man, but also a gentle and generous one. Such a man was the English king Richard I. He was called Richard the Lion-Heart and bore three lions on his shield.

"Birds, fish, insects, mammals, flowers, fruit, and even objects like spoons, bells, ladders, castles—I know not where to stop—can be found on coats of arms. A king once rewarded his prize chef with an honorary coat of arms—a shield decorated with three cooking pots.

COOKING POTS
The shield of the great French chef Taillevent, who cooked for the court of Charles V in the 1300s.

THE SCALADO
The scalado is a scaling ladder used to climb over castle walls in an attack.

THE FLEA
The flea is said to appear in an Italian family's coat of arms.

"Besides the dragon, imaginary creatures were much used—unicorns, two-headed eagles, gryphons,● and mermaids, to name a few.

THE COCKATRICE
A cockatrice is a form of dragon. Ancient myth claims the cockatrice came from an egg laid by a nine-year-old rooster and hatched by a toad on a dunghill.

THE UNICORN
As late as the 1600s, many people believed that unicorns really existed.

THE PELICAN
Myth has it that the female pelican, when shown in the nest with her young, is drawing blood from her chest to feed them.

● Monsters that are part eagle and part lion

"All the heraldic symbols I have described would be of little worth without an artist to put them to use for all to see. Artists painted designs on shields, embroidered them on banners and garments, and sculpted them on medallions and helmet crests. The father of Jean Froissart, the fourteenth-century French writer, was such an artist. A painter of arms, ● he was called.

"A family being given a coat of arms from the king would suggest to the artist the design they wanted. If they were great hunters, they might want a wild boar or stag in their design. Ho! A bowlegged knight, said to resemble a crab in his walk, had a crab on his shield. Centuries later, his descendants, bowlegged or not, bore that same crab in the family coat of arms.

"The artist had to follow a few basic rules about color. One of the metals—gold or silver—was supposed to appear somewhere on every shield. If both appeared, one should not be on top of the other. Nor were colors to be placed on top of each other.

"All designs had to be approved by the king of heralds. ●

● Short for *coat of arms*, not to be confused with *arms* meaning weapons or *arms* meaning limbs of the body
● The chief herald of a large area that includes many towns and villages Today England has three kings of heralds, also called kings of arms.

"At heraldry's headquarters—a royal building set aside for heraldic study and development—Harold the pursuivant spent much time memorizing the coats of arms recorded there. This headquarters would later be known as the College of Arms.

"Some of the designs, or devices (as they are also called) were kept on rolls of parchment. Others were simply described in books, in Blazon. Harold was beginning to read Blazon quite well.

THE MAIN COLOR OF A SHIELD UPON WHICH THE DESIGN IS PLACED IS CALLED THE FIELD.

IN BLAZON THE FIELD'S COLOR IS ALWAYS GIVEN TO US FIRST.

GULES, A MULLET ● ARGENT =

WHEW! I LOVE TO STUDY, BUT I CAN'T WAIT TO GET OUTSIDE AND PLAY THROWING THE BAR! ●

● Blazon for *star*
● A game where players compete to see who can throw a long, thick bar of iron or wood the farthest. The distance was measured in lengths of the bar. Harold was strong and was a match for any of the competing young heralds, squires, and knights.

111

"When Harold read, 'Per pale ● or and vert, a lion rampant ● gules,' he saw in his mind—

the shield of possibly the greatest tournament champion ever—William Marshal, Earl of Pembroke.

"The words, 'Gules, a lion passant guardant ● or' brought to Harold's mind—

the arms of Eleanor of Aquitaine. She was twice married, first to a French king and then to an English king, and was the mother of Richard the Lion-Heart.

● Divided vertically down the middle
● Rearing up and standing on the left hind leg with forepaws extended
● The bend is red where it lies on silver and silver where it lies on red.
● Walking, right paw raised, with full face turned toward you

"Upon reading, 'Per pale argent and gules, a bend counterchanged,' ● he would imagine—

the shield of Geoffrey Chaucer, the fourteenth-century poet.

"If he read, 'Argent a pile gules,' he saw—

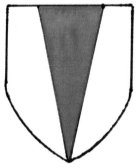

the arms of the fourteenth-century English knight, Sir John Chandos.

"Upon reading the words, 'Argent two bars and in chief three mullets gules,' Harold would see—

the shield of George Washington's fourteenth-century ancestors.

"You may have heard of King Arthur, Sir Lancelot, and the other knights of the Round Table. Did they truly exist? Today many believe they were just legends, make-believe. In Harold's day, there were no such doubts. Everyone, including Harold, believed in these heroes, who were said to have lived and performed their brave feats of arms eight hundred years before Harold was born.

"When Harold looked for King Arthur's original coat of arms in the headquarters of heraldry, he could find no single official record. Instead he found many coats of arms for King Arthur. Different artists had made up what they thought King Arthur's coat of arms should be and painted their designs in books and on the walls of palaces and churches.

"A noble family's coat of arms was more personal and more treasured even than its name. The privilege of having a coat of arms was not limited to royalty and nobility, however. Rich merchants, bankers, landowners, and even successful artists could be granted coats of arms by the king. This was considered a high honor. It meant they were receiving from the crown the same important regard given to knights, lords, bishops, dukes, and so forth.

"Many families and individuals not deemed by the crown worthy of coats of arms simply faked them and put them over their doors and on their dishes, silverware, and other personal belongings.

"Like a detective, Harold the pursuivant was often sent out by Prince Lionel to search for these culprits, who were breaking the law. These searches were called visitations.

"One day an excited Harold received his first military assignment. He would observe a battle with Prince Lionel's older herald. Although heralds were protected by a code that forbade their being attacked, the two men still wore chain-mail armor under their tabards and stood a safe distance from the fighting. Their job was to watch closely the behavior of Prince Lionel's knights as they fought the French. Did a knight perform valiant feats of arms, or was he cowardly? Above all, did a knight behave in a chivalrous manner—did he honor the rules of battle and knighthood, show dignity and mercy?

Behave bravely

"Harold and Edward reported what they saw to Prince Lionel. Prince Lionel would reward a brave knight with more money, more promotions, and more attention at court than one who was not so brave.

"After a battle, it was the custom for the heralds of both sides to decide who was the official winner. They counted the bodies strewn about the field amid dead horses, twisted shields, ruined armor. The side with the least dead was usually declared the victor.

"After the battle of Agincourt, in 1415, the number of English dead was put at around one hundred and the French dead at between seven and ten thousand. Even though it was obvious to all that the English were the victors, a French herald had to declare it to the English king before it became official. Records of these victories and defeats were kept by the heralds. On a monument to the great Scots knight Lord Douglas, his record is engraved: 'Thirteen times he was defeated in battle, fifty-seven times victorious.'

"There was no end to the variety of duties Harold the pursuivant was soon performing. Knights were known for their bravery and strength, heralds for their bravery and brains. They were called the 'professors of chivalry.' ●

"Before a battle Harold would write down the words and wishes of many of the knights. Such a record served as a knight's will and made certain his family would legally inherit his lands and money if he were killed.

"Harold also carried important messages to both friends and foes of Prince Lionel. Sometimes the messages were written. Often they were memorized instead, even though they might be so long that it took Harold fifteen or twenty minutes to recite them. Memorized messages could not fall into the wrong hands, but written messages could. A pursuivant's or a herald's safety in enemy territory was guaranteed by all sides. Sadly, the guarantees were not always honored, and heralds did occasionally die while delivering messages.

● Experts in the rules, traditions, and history that governed knights' behavior

"When a herald was in an enemy's camp, sometimes even within the enemy's castle walls, he was treated as a guest. While awaiting a reply to the message he had brought, he was fed well and entertained. When a herald left, it was the custom for the enemy leaders to give him many fine gifts in honor of the service the herald was performing for both sides, and probably also to win a bit of his friendship and make it difficult for the herald to dislike his host.

"You see, while amongst the enemy, a herald was not supposed to spy, but ho!—some did. A herald might notice a weakened part of a castle wall, or a shortage of catapults,  or bad morale among the foot soldiers. Upon his return home, a dishonest herald might report this to his leaders. Unchivalrous it was. Woe to the spying herald if ever he were caught by the enemy.

● Big slingshots that could throw one-hundred-pound rocks
● Blazon for *sprinkled*
● Blazon for *checkered*

"Heralds also acted as what you today might call publicists. The knight William Marshal, the greatest tournament winner of almost eight hundred years ago, was said by his detractors to have had his reputation much inflated by his noisy herald, Henry le Norreis. All heralds sang out the praises of their masters and exaggerated their accomplishments, but le Norreis was the boldest. At every tournament he could be heard outshouting the other heralds, crying, 'Make way for the Marshal!' and 'God aid the Marshal!'

● This is true.

"In medieval days there was great interest in heraldry among all the people. Every now and then, much to the professional heralds' chagrin, an accomplished amateur came along who had become a master of heraldry by studying on his own.

"There was a certain English duke—I forget his name—who, when he needed someone to identify the oncoming enemy and assess its strengths and weaknesses, entrusted the task not to his herald but to his barber!

These are made-up names and coats of arms.

"Heralds were much involved in planning and running jousts, or tournaments, the most popular sport of Harold's day. Heralds helped decide which knights were qualified to enter; they kept score; gave the signal to start or stop each event; and, like referees or umpires today, enforced the rules. One absolute rule of jousting was that all lances must be the same length and weight—swords and maces, also.

"At his first tournament, Harold the pursuivant acted like a sports announcer. He stood behind the noble ladies and gentlemen in Prince Lionel's stand and told them in a loud, excited voice who each knight was, where he was from, and what his past tournament record was. He also explained some of the finer points of the action.

"On the lighter side, Harold the pursuivant often carried love letters back and forth between noblemen and ladies of Prince Lionel's court. They knew Harold was trustworthy and would not blabbe or gossib ● about them. If the romance led to marriage, Harold would very likely be asked to arrange the entire ceremony from choosing the flowers and music to arranging the seating of the guests—and much more. For this he was handsomely rewarded.

"Not on the lighter side, heralds also sometimes arranged funerals, from the church ceremony to the funeral procession to the burial.

● Medieval for *blab* or *gossip*

"After several years of apprenticeship, during which he served Prince Lionel well, Harold the pursuivant became Harold the Herald.

"In honor of Harold's new position, the prince gave him many fine gifts including a house and land. At the high point of the ceremony, the prince personally poured wine over Harold's head. He then gave Harold the cup—and a towaille, ● I would assume.

"Harold the Herald would now receive the same comfortable wage as most knights and, like them, would pay no taxes. It was considered that knights paid their taxes to their sovereign by defending him from his enemies. Heralds, too, were a part of a sovereign's defense.

"Harold married, had three children, and in time became a king of heralds.

"Thank ou, Godd blesse ou, and may wee meete agayne." ●

● Medieval for *towel*
● Medieval for *"Thank you, God bless you, and may we meet again."*

As the students leave the auditorium, the guard and armor give each class a poster of a coat of arms to hang on their classroom wall.

929.8   Fradon, Dana.
F
        Harold the herald.

$14.95

DATE			
FE 9 '96			
MY 18 '98			

BAKER & TAYLOR